# FELICITY DISCOVERS A SECRET

FELICITY · 1774

BY VALERIE TRIPP

ILLUSTRATIONS DAN ANDREASEN

VIGNETTES DAN ANDREASEN, PHILIP HOOD

THE AMERICAN GIRLS COLLECTION®

Published by Pleasant Company Publications
Previously published in *American Girl* magazine
Copyright © 2002 by Pleasant Company

For information, address: Book Editor, Pleasant Company Publications,
8400 Fairway Place, P.O. Box 620998, Middleton, WI 53562.

Visit our Web site at **americangirl.com**

Printed in Singapore.
02 03 04 05 06 07 08 09 TWP 10 9 8 7 6 5 4 3 2 1

The American Girls Collection® and logo, American Girls Short Stories,™
the American Girl logo, Felicity,® and Felicity Merriman®
are trademarks of Pleasant Company.

**Library of Congress Cataloging-in-Publication Data**

Tripp, Valerie, 1951–
Felicity discovers a secret / by Valerie Tripp ;
illustrations, Dan Andreasen; vignettes, Philip Hood.
p. cm. — (The American girls collection)
Summary: In 1776 Williamsburg, Virginia, Felicity helps
the irritable Mrs. Burnie do laundry and learns a secret
that seems to explain her behavior. Includes notes on the
history of eyeglasses and instructions for making a pair of
lorgnettes, glass lenses attached to elegant handles.

ISBN 1-58485-477-4
[1. Secrets—Fiction. 2. Visually handicapped—Fiction. 3.
Physically handicapped—Fiction. 4. Eyeglasses—Fiction.
5. Prejudices—Fiction. 6. Virginia—Social life and cus-
toms—to 1775—Fiction. 7. Williamsburg (Va.)—Fiction.]
I. Andreasen, Dan, ill. II. Hood, Philip, ill. III. Title. IV. Series.
PZ7.T7363 Fc 2002    [Fic]—dc21    2001036658

# The AMERICAN GIRLS COLLECTION™

PICTURE CREDITS
The following individuals and organizations have generously given
permission to reprint illustrations contained in "Looking Back":
p. 31—Courtesy of J. William Rosenthal, M.D.; p. 32—Pierre Marly; p. 33—© CORBIS;
1300s eyeglasses, Pierre Marly; p. 34—© Bettmann/CORBIS; p. 35—Engraving by
Mauron, published by Tempest, 1711; p. 36—© CORBIS; p. 37—© 1996 Archive
Photos/Picture Quest; p. 38—Photo courtesy of the Museum of Vision, Foundation
for the American Academy of Ophthalmology; p. 39—© Michael Keller/The Stock
Market; p. 40—Photography by Jamie Young and craft by June Pratt.

# TABLE OF CONTENTS

## FELICITY'S FAMILY AND FRIENDS

# FELICITY'S FAMILY

### FATHER
*Felicity's father, who owns one of the general stores in Williamsburg.*

### MOTHER
*Felicity's mother, who takes care of her family with love and pride.*

### FELICITY
*A spunky, spritely colonial girl, growing up just before the American Revolution.*

**NAN**
*Felicity's sweet and
sensible sister, who is
six years old.*

**WILLIAM**
*Felicity's three-year-old
brother, who likes mischief
and mud puddles.*

**MRS. BURNIE**
*A fussy and
disapproving woman
who repairs embroidery
and washes linens.*

# FELICITY DISCOVERS
## A SECRET

Faster, faster, *faster,* Felicity ran as she rolled her hoop along the sidewalk. After weeks of cold, dreary rain, the sun was shining and a strong spring breeze was shooing winter's last gray clouds out of the sky. The ground was muddy and the streets were full of puddles to dodge, but Felicity didn't mind. She was so glad to be out-of-doors!

She gave her hoop another tap with her stick to make it spin faster. The hoop

picked up speed and
raced ahead so fast,
it hardly seemed to
touch the ground at all.
Felicity grinned and ran to catch up with
it. Before she could, the hoop hit a stone,
skipped up into the air, and landed—
*splash!*—in the middle of a big, messy
puddle, splattering mud all over some
linen sheets that had been spread on
bushes to dry in the sun. Felicity dove
at the hoop to grab it, but she only made
things worse by crashing into the bushes
herself. Linens flopped into the puddle,
and Felicity landed splat on top of them!

Felicity looked at herself. Her skirt
was soaked through and her stockings

were dotted with globs of mud. But that
wasn't the worst of it.

"You there!" cried a voice, and
Felicity's heart sank straight to the bottom
of her soggy shoes. She realized that these
were not just *any* linens she had spoiled.
These linens were on bushes in front of
Mrs. Burnie's house. Mrs. Burnie repaired
embroidery for the milliner and took in
fine linens to launder. She was famous for
being fussy.

Mrs. Burnie flew toward Felicity now,
scolding as she came. "Merciful heavens,
what a miserable mess!" she said. "Look
what you've done, you thoughtless,
blundering girl!"

Felicity stood up and tried to wipe

*"Merciful heavens, what a miserable mess!" said Mrs. Burnie.*
*"Look what you've done, you thoughtless, blundering girl!"*

4

the mud off her hands but only smeared it across her skirt. "I'm sorry, Mrs. Burnie," she said.

Felicity felt a little scared. She had heard the gossip about Mrs. Burnie. People said she couldn't get along with anyone because she was so opinionated and so dead set against change. She wore clothing that had gone out of style years ago. She had disapproved so much when they added the new bell tower to the church that she had frowned through every service since. Everyone said she was peculiar, and indeed she did look a bit odd. Her apron was on inside out, and her hair was lopsided, as if she had pinned it up without looking. Felicity tried not to stare as she apologized again, "I'm very, very sorry. Please forgive me."

"Pretty words," scoffed Mrs. Burnie. She lifted a muddy napkin out of the puddle with two fingers and frowned. "Be off with you now!" she said. "I promised these linens would be ready by tomorrow, so I've a great deal of work to do, thanks to your clumsiness."

"Shall I help you?" Felicity asked meekly, stooping to gather the rest of the muddy cloths from the ground.

"No! Go away!" said Mrs. Burnie. "You've caused enough trouble. And look at you, covered with mud. What help could you be?"

Felicity handed the muddy linens to Mrs. Burnie. She felt terrible about the mess she'd made. She knew what she ought to do—what her parents would say she must do. So though it was the last thing she *wanted* to do, she said, "I'll come back tomorrow, then, and help."

Mrs. Burnie hesitated. She squinted at Felicity as if she were sizing her up. "I don't like people hanging about," she said, scowling. "But the work must be done. So come early and I'll put you to work—nuisance though it'll be to have you around!"

"Yes, ma'am," said Felicity.

"Fuss and bother!" Mrs. Burnie muttered as she turned away.

Home Felicity trudged, dragging her hoop and stick and feeling very sorry for herself. She had to spend the next day with Mrs. Burnie, the prickliest lady in Williamsburg. It was sure to be terrible!

And terrible it was, at first. When Felicity arrived early in the morning, Mrs. Burnie was waiting for her. Today Mrs. Burnie's apron was on right side out, but her cap was backward. She seemed already out of patience.

"Come along," she said. "You moved quick enough yesterday when you were rolling your hoop. We'll see if you move as fast when you're working. Follow me."

She led Felicity around to the back of her house, where there was a small yard.

"Fetch wood from the pile, build a fire under the cauldron, and fill the cauldron with water from the well," ordered Mrs. Burnie. "When the water heats up, put the dirty linen in the cauldron, scrub it with soap, and stir it with this paddle. Do you understand?"

"Yes, ma'am," answered Felicity.

And so the drudgery began. Felicity walked back and forth carrying armloads of wood, then back and forth carrying buckets of water. The work was hard and dull. Mrs. Burnie made a fuss about everything from the size of the fire to the way Felicity rubbed soap on the linens.

"Hold the soap like *this,*" Mrs. Burnie said, putting it in Felicity's hand.

Felicity looked at the soap. "I've never seen such a big cake of soap before," she said. "This isn't like the soap my mother uses."

"I make my soap myself," said Mrs. Burnie. "Always have

10

and always will. It's pure foolishness to buy soap at the store the way some do nowadays. Mind you rub the soap onto every single piece of linen."

"My mother does it differently," Felicity said. "Her way is easier. She makes the water sudsy, and then—"

"I do it the way I've always done it," said Mrs. Burnie firmly, cutting off all discussion. "Different isn't better."

After Felicity scrubbed and stirred the linens in the cauldron, Mrs. Burnie directed her to rinse them over and over again in cool water until the rinse water ran clear. Then Felicity had to twist each piece of linen hard to wring the water out. By the time she carefully spread the linens on boxwood bushes to dry, her arms and shoulders ached with tiredness.

"There," said Felicity when the last cloth was spread on the last bush. "What comes next?"

"Let's hope no hoops!" said Mrs. Burnie.

Felicity glanced up and was surprised to see that Mrs. Burnie was smiling a little. Felicity smiled back. *Mrs. Burnie is fussy, and she dislikes anything new,* she thought. *There's no denying that. But she is rather nice, too.*

"Come along inside now, and we'll iron while these dry," said Mrs. Burnie.

The inside of Mrs. Burnie's house was tidy, but as she looked around, Felicity noticed a few things that seemed odd.

Some of the books on the shelf were
upside down, and a painting hung sideways on the wall. Felicity saw a label
Mrs. Burnie had written on a jar
of spice, and she was surprised
to see that Mrs. Burnie's handwriting was as large and scrawly
as a young child's.

Felicity also saw a beautiful piece of
embroidery draped over the arm of a
chair by the window. "Oh, how lovely!"
she said, running her hand over it gently.
"The stitches are so tiny and perfect."
Felicity picked up the embroidery and
looked at it closely. "That's odd," she
said. "Why is this flower upside down,
not like all the others?"

*"That's odd," Felicity said. "Why is this flower upside down, not like all the others?"*

"What?" said Mrs. Burnie. Quickly, she took the embroidery out of Felicity's hands and held it close to her face for a moment. "Oh, dear," she sighed to herself unhappily. Her shoulders sagged, and she seemed lost in her thoughts. Then, as if suddenly remembering that Felicity was there, she put the embroidery down and said sharply, "Bring me that basket of napkins to be ironed. We've work to do."

Felicity was not surprised to find that Mrs. Burnie was just as particular about ironing as she was about washing.

"You must spread the napkin out like this," Mrs. Burnie instructed. "And you must fold it like this." She ran her hands over every napkin after Felicity had ironed it, carefully checking for wrinkles and mismatched edges. "This one is not good enough," she said more than once. "You will have to do it over."

Despite everything, Felicity found herself beginning to enjoy the work. There was something curiously pleasing about it. Once, Mrs. Burnie whisked a napkin from Felicity and with her own quick, sure hands folded it and ironed it smooth.

"Oh, you make it look so easy!" said Felicity with admiration. "You do it perfectly without even looking!"

"Ah, well, my hands have done this hundreds of times," said Mrs. Burnie with an odd little smile. "It's my job. It's what

I am paid to do. If I don't do my ironing and embroidery perfectly, I won't be paid. And if I'm not paid, I don't eat. It's that simple."

When the big, snowy white sheets were dry, Mrs. Burnie showed Felicity how to iron and fold them—edges matching exactly, of course!—and how to slip sprigs of lavender between the folds.

Felicity took a deep breath. "Mmm! The lavender smells nice," she said.

"Aye," said Mrs. Burnie, pleased. "When you sleep on sheets that smell of lavender, you're sure to have sweet dreams."

"Oh, but you're almost out of

lavender!" Felicity said. "The basket is nearly empty."

"It is?" said Mrs. Burnie. She felt the bottom of the basket with her hand. "Indeed, you're right."

"I have lavender in my garden," said Felicity eagerly. "Would you like to come home with me and cut some? I know my mother would be happy to have you stay to tea."

"No, I don't think so," Mrs. Burnie answered, not unkindly but quite firmly. "I'm not much of a one for visiting these days. I stay close to home. Now, mind you don't wrinkle that sheet!"

At long last the end of the day came.

All the linens Felicity and her hoop had muddied were rewashed, redried, ironed, folded neatly, and tied in stacks with smooth blue ribbons. Felicity thought they looked like perfection itself. She felt tired but happy.

"Go on home now. Go bother some-one else," Mrs. Burnie said, smiling. "You're not such a bad child after all."

"And you're not . . ." Felicity stopped.

Mrs. Burnie laughed and finished for her. "And I'm not such a terrible, mean old lady!"

"Now that I have spent time with you, I think you are very nice," said Felicity.

"You've a winning way about you," said Mrs. Burnie. "But go on now. And be careful with that hoop of yours!"

"I will," promised Felicity, grinning. "Good-bye!"

❧

The next morning Felicity was up early. She hurried to her garden, gathered a big bunch of lavender, and ran to Mrs. Burnie's house to surprise her. *Oh, won't Mrs. Burnie be pleased with me!* she thought, very pleased indeed with herself.

She knocked on Mrs. Burnie's front door. When no one answered, she went around to the back, but Mrs. Burnie wasn't outside, either. So Felicity peeked

in the window. She saw Mrs. Burnie in her chair, bent so far forward her face seemed to be touching her embroidery. *Oh, she's asleep,* Felicity thought. *I'll just go in and leave the lavender for her as a surprise.*

But as Felicity tiptoed in, she saw that Mrs. Burnie was not asleep after all. She was stitching her embroidery—with her face almost touching the cloth. "Good day, Mrs. Burnie," Felicity said.

Mrs. Burnie's head jerked up, and she cried out as if she were frightened. "Who is it?" she asked. Then she blinked and said crossly, "Oh, Felicity. It's you. What do you want?"

"I brought some lavender," said Felicity.

"Well, put it down and then go," said Mrs. Burnie coldly. "What were you thinking of, sneaking in without knocking?"

"I'm sorry!" said Felicity. "I didn't mean to disturb you. I looked in the window and I thought you were asleep. Why do you lean so close to your embroidery?"

"*Go!*" ordered Mrs. Burnie. She was truly angry now. "Don't come back. I don't want to see you here ever again. Ever!"

Felicity dropped the lavender and fled. Out of the room, out of the house, down the street, all the way back to her garden she ran, tears of hurt and confusion streaking her cheeks. She flung herself on a bench, out of breath. *What did I do to make Mrs. Burnie so angry?* she wondered. *I thought we were friends!*

As she calmed herself, Felicity thought hard. She remembered all the odd things she had noticed about Mrs. Burnie: her inside-out apron, her lopsided hair, her backward cap, her upside-down books, her sideways painting, her large handwriting, the odd flower in her embroidery, the way she inspected the linens with her hands, the way she was leaning over her embroidery this morning, the way she avoided people . . .

Suddenly it all made sense to Felicity. Mrs. Burnie had a secret. There was something she did not want people to know, because she was afraid she would lose her job if they did.

Felicity had an idea. She knew a way to help Mrs. Burnie. She made up her mind to do it. She stood up, brushed away her tears, and set forth for her father's store.

This time when Felicity knocked on the door, Mrs. Burnie answered.

"Oh, I'm glad you came back," she said. "I'm sorry I was so cross before."

"Mrs. Burnie," Felicity said slowly, "I think I know why you were cross."

"You do?"

"Yes," said Felicity. "I believe I know your secret now. I think perhaps you need these." Felicity brought her hand from behind her back and held out a pair of eyeglasses.

"I borrowed them from my father's store," Felicity explained. "He sells used eyeglasses." Felicity took a deep breath and went on. "I know you don't like changes, but some new things are good," she said. "Please try them. They'll help you with your embroidery."

Mrs. Burnie paused. "I don't know," she said. "Eyeglasses . . . I've thought of them, but I've never heard of a lady wearing them."

"Oh, things have changed!" exclaimed Felicity. "It isn't so unusual anymore for ladies to wear eyeglasses at home. Please don't refuse to try them just because they're different. Sometimes different *is* better."

Mrs. Burnie took the eyeglasses from Felicity and slowly, slowly put them on. As soon as she did, her face lit up. She smiled at Felicity, then hurried inside and picked up her embroidery. Behind the glasses, her eyes were bright. "Oh!" she said, delighted. "These *do* help!"

Felicity grinned. "Please promise you'll get a pair for yourself," she said.

"I will," said Mrs. Burnie. "Thank you, Felicity." Then she grinned, too. "My goodness," she said. "How extraordinary! Here I am with two new things in one week. They make a world of difference, and I am pleased as can be with both of them—my new eyeglasses *and* my new friend!"

# VALERIE TRIPP

At 9          Now

One day, when I was having a hard time threading a needle, I realized that I needed eyeglasses. Just like Mrs. Burnie, I am delighted with the difference eyeglasses have made!

*Valerie Tripp has written forty-four books in The American Girls Collection, including ten about Felicity.*

LOOKING
BACK
1774

# A PEEK INTO
# THE PAST

In Felicity's time, people didn't go to eye doctors for eye exams or for prescriptions for eyeglasses. Instead, shops like Mr. Merriman's sold new and used glasses over the counter. Customers simply tried on glasses until they found ones that helped them see better—and fit their faces!

Most of the glasses sold in the late 1700s were temple eyeglasses imported from Europe. The first temple glasses had arms ending in

*Temple glasses with green lenses to protect eyes from the sun*

flat rings. The rings pressed against the temples, holding the glasses in place. A later version of temple glasses had hinged arms that wrapped around the head and folded down for storage.

Wealthy people in both Europe and America had eyeglasses made especially for them. Some frames had intricate designs carved on them. Others were made from gold or ivory and were studded with jewels. Some custom-made lenses weren't framed at all but were hidden in fans or walking sticks.

*A fan with a hidden eyepiece*

The fanciest eyeglasses of the era were *lorgnettes* (lorn-YETS), or glass lenses attached to elegant handles. Women who needed glasses carried lorgnettes so that they could look as fashionable as possible. Lorgnettes also helped give women a better view at the theater or the opera—where observing other people was sometimes more entertaining than the show!

People probably began wearing eyeglasses in Europe in the 1200s, but no one knows for sure when or where they were invented. Scholars and writers began wearing eyeglasses when they couldn't see clearly enough to read or write. They wore eyeglasses with *convex lenses,* which were thicker in the middle than at the edges. These lenses worked best for *farsighted* people—those who had trouble seeing nearby images, such as words in a book.

The earliest eyeglasses with convex lenses were made by riveting together the handles of two magnifying glasses. The wearers held them in front of their eyes or balanced them on their noses, but any movement sent the lenses falling!

*Eyeglasses from the late 1300s*

33

In the 1300s, most people couldn't read or write and didn't need perfect vision to do their work, so eyeglasses were rare. But in the mid-1400s, the printing press was invented. As printed material became available, more people learned to read and realized they needed eyeglasses to help them. But reading was still not for everyone.

*Johannes Gutenberg, inventor of the printing press, holds his first printed sheet.*

Only the upper classes learned to read, and wearing glasses became a sign of wealth.

In the 1500s, spectacle makers created eyeglasses for *nearsighted* people, or people who had trouble seeing objects that were far away. These glasses had *concave lenses,* which were thicker at the edges than in the middle and made faraway objects appear clearer. Now glasses could be worn for outdoor activities, such as hunting.

By the 1600s, eyeglasses were becoming more common. Street peddlers and shopkeepers in big cities throughout Europe displayed trays of inexpensive glasses that people of any class could afford. Eyeglasses were no longer only for the wealthy.

Temple eyeglasses hadn't been invented yet, so people still held their glasses in front of their eyes when they needed to read or look closely at something. People also devised ways to wear glasses without having to hold them. They rigged the frames with ribbons or leather straps that tied around their ears or behind their heads.

*Straps around the ears held these glasses on.*

By Felicity's time, people were wearing glasses with ease, but there was still progress to be made. People who needed help seeing both close-up and faraway objects had to switch back and forth between two pairs of glasses. In 1784, Benjamin Franklin solved this problem by cutting lenses in half. He put the concave lenses in the top of his frames and the convex lenses in the bottom. With these glasses, he could look up to see objects that were

*Benjamin Franklin*

far away and down to see objects close by.

After this invention, Benjamin Franklin wrote to a friend, "I could not distinguish a Letter even of Large Print; but am happy in the invention of Double Spectacles, which serving for distant objects as well as near ones, make my Eyes as useful to me as they ever were." Today, glasses that help people see both near and far away are called *bifocals.*

It wasn't until the late 1800s that doctors and scientists began to under-stand the workings of the human eye. They learned to correct nearsightedness, farsightedness, and more

*In the late 1800s, doctors used **ophthalmometers** (ahf-thal-MOM-uh-durs) like this one to examine eyes.*

serious vision problems. They were also able to give their patients thorough vision exams and to write prescriptions for customized lenses.

Another major advancement in the late 1800s was the invention of contact lenses. The first contact lenses, introduced in 1887, were large and uncomfortable and could only be worn for short stretches of time. Today's contact lenses are much more comfortable, but many people still prefer to

*Modern-day contact lenses*

make a fashion statement with a unique pair of eyeglasses—just as people did in Felicity's time.

# MAKE LORGNETTES

*What do you see with your fancy eyeglasses?*

When Felicity was a girl, lorgnettes were a fashion statement. These hand-held eyeglasses were the fanciest of the era. They had handles of gold, silver, mother-of-pearl, or tortoiseshell. Many of them were adorned with jewels.

Make a fancy pair of lorgnettes, and see what you can see!

## YOU WILL NEED:

♥ *An adult to help you*
*Tracing paper, 8½ by 11 inches*
*Pencil*
*Newspaper*
*Poster board, 8½ by 11 inches*
*Scissors*
*Thumbtack*
*Brass paper fastener*
*Tape*
*Glue*
*Colored pencils, markers, or paints*
*Decorations such as sequins, glitter, and ribbon*

1. Use the tracing paper and pencil to trace the patterns from the back of this book. Trace the handle pattern twice. Mark the dots at the top of the patterns.

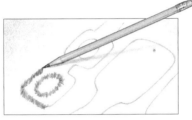

2. Place the tracing paper onto newspaper, design side down. Use the side of the pencil lead to color over the lines and dots on the back of each pattern.

**3.** Place the tracing paper on the poster board, design side up. Draw over the lines of the patterns, pressing firmly.

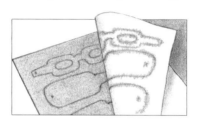

**4.** Lift the tracing paper. The pencil markings from the back of the paper will come off where you traced.

**5.** Cut out the eyeglasses and 2 handles. Have an adult cut out the insides of the eyeglasses.

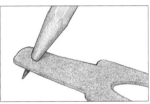

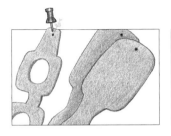

6. Use a thumbtack to carefully make holes at the dots. Then use a sharp pencil to make the holes a bit bigger.

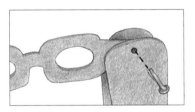

7. Place the eyeglass piece between the 2 handles. Insert the brass paper fastener through all 3 holes.

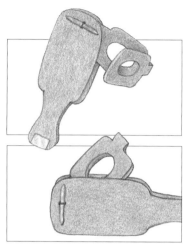

**8.** Tape the handles together at the bottom. Fold the eyeglasses in half at the nose-piece and tuck them into the handle.

**9.** Decorate your lorgnettes to make them as fancy as you like!

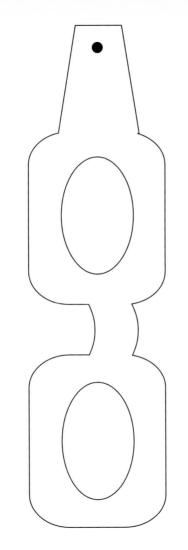

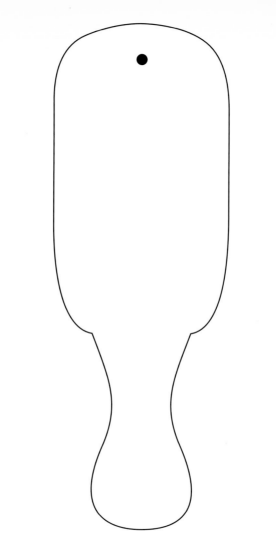